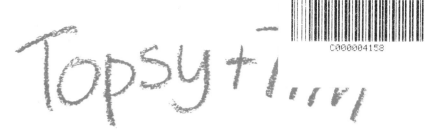

meet the babysitter

Jean and Gareth Adamson

Blackie

C000004158

Copyright © 1989 Jean and Gareth Adamson
First published in 1989 by Blackie and Son Limited
Reprinted 1991

All rights reserved. No part of this publication
may be reproduced, stored in a retrieval system,
or transmitted in any form or by any means,
electronic, mechanical, photocopying, recording
or otherwise without the written permission
of the Publishers.

British Library Cataloguing in Publication Data
Adamson, Jean, 1928–
Topsy and Tim meet the babysitter
I. Title   II. Adamson, Gareth, 1925–1982
823' 914[J]

ISBN 0-216-92593-2
ISBN 0-216-92592-4 Pbk

Blackie and Son Limited
7 Leicester Place
London WC2H 7BP

Printed in Portugal

Topsy and Tim's Mummy and Dad
were getting ready to go to a party.
It was a party for grown-ups, so
Topsy and Tim were not invited.
'It's not fair,' said Tim.

'You'll be all right,' said Dad.
'Mummy knows a very nice babysitter
called Linda. She is coming
to look after you while we are out.'

'We don't need a babysitter,'
said Topsy. 'We are not babies.'
'If you are going to be naughty,'
said Mummy, 'Dad and I will not
be able to go to the party.'

Mummy and Dad didn't often go to parties.
Topsy and Tim had been to lots.

They helped make sandwiches
for Linda's supper and they
promised to put themselves
to bed at seven.

When Linda arrived
Mummy and Dad left for the party.
Topsy and Tim waved goodbye
and called, 'Have a nice time.'
Mummy and Dad called back,
'Be good.'

'What would you like to do
until bedtime?' asked Linda.
'Mummy left some video cartoons
to watch,' said Topsy.

Linda didn't know how the video worked,
but Topsy and Tim soon showed her.
Then they all sat and watched
the funny cartoon films together.

When the video was finished
Linda switched it off.
'Now I'll make your bedtime drink,'
she said.
Linda made their favourite bedtime drink
and Roly Poly had a little drink too.

'We helped Mummy make some
sandwiches for your supper, Linda,'
said Tim.
'They do look tasty,' said Linda.
'I shall enjoy them later, when
you are in bed.'

Just then the telephone rang.
Linda answered it. She began
to explain that Mummy and Dad
were out at a party.

While she was speaking on the
phone Topsy and Tim heard the
clock strike seven.
'That's our bedtime,' whispered
Topsy. 'Let's give Linda a surprise.'

They tiptoed upstairs to the bathroom, washed themselves, cleaned their teeth and got into their pyjamas.

Then they should have got into
bed—but they didn't. Instead
they crept into their bedroom
and hid behind the door.

Downstairs Linda was looking
for Topsy and Tim.
'Wherever can they be?' she said.
Roly Poly led her upstairs.

She guessed they had put
themselves to bed, but when
she looked in their bedroom
their beds were empty.

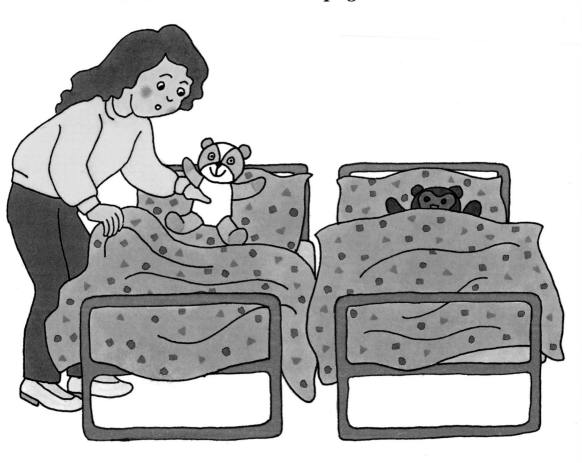

Linda was puzzled, then she said
in a loud voice,
'If Topsy and Tim are not in bed
by the time I have counted to five,
NO BEDTIME STORY.
One...Two...Three...Four...'

Before she could say 'Five,'
Topsy and Tim burst out from
their hiding place behind the
bedroom door.
'WE WANT A BEDTIME STORY!'
they shouted as they jumped into
their beds.

Linda sat beside them and read
their favourite bedtime story.
Linda was a good story reader.

By the time she had finished
Topsy and Tim were almost asleep.
She tucked them in and went quietly
downstairs to wait for Mummy and Dad.

When Mummy and Dad came home they tiptoed into Topsy and Tim's bedroom. Topsy opened one eye.
'Did you have a nice time?' she asked.
'Lovely,' said Mummy.
'So did we,' said Topsy—and went back to sleep.